WRITTEN BY ERIN BRERETON

HILARY ROCKS!

ON STAGE, SCREEN, AND IN BETWEEN, HILARY DUFF IS LIVING A FAIRY TALE LIFE!

TRIUMPH ENTERTAINMENT
Division of Triumph Books
601 South LaSalle Street
Chicago, Illinois 60605

Role of a Lifetime

Hilary as Cinderella? What a perfect match!

Hilary Duff's wacky, lighthearted Lizzie McGuire role made her famous. But even though the 16-year-old made a name for herself playing the girl next door, she was eager to take on a very different role: that of a modern day Cinderella, in A Cinderella Story.

After all, her character in the movie, Sam, isn't your average fairy princess in disguise.

"This is really an updated version of the story, and this is probably the most girl-empowered Cinderella we've seen in the movies," Hilary told Billboard.

There's more girl power than nervous giggles in A Cinderella Story.

"If you look at all the other Cinderella stories, the girl is kind of passive," Duff has said. "Even though it's a great, beautiful story that everyone fell in love with, she doesn't really fight for herself. She kind of waits for things to fall into place and waits for Prince Charming to come and sweep her off of her feet."

"Sam definitely gets support from her friends, but she's very independent, a strong, sensible type of person," Duff said. "Even though she might not be the prettiest girl in school and everyone overlooks her, she still wants to succeed. She's a fighter. Then the guy comes, which is the good park. But she gets what she wants because she fights for it."

4

almost famous

BEFORE HILARY STARRED AS A MODERN-DAY CINDERELLA, SHE PLAYED A NUMBER OF OTHER CHARACTERS IN TV SHOWS AND MOVIES!

star struggles

18 19

FAMILY TIES

22 23

the many loves of Hilary Duff

Hil's love life is almost as hectic as her filming schedule!

Hilary Duff has already achieved fame (she's made hit songs and hit movies!) and fortune (how many other teens do you know who've bought a mansion?) – now she's got one more horizon to conquer: boys!

Not that Hilary hasn't been logging in some serious guy time. The 16-year-old cutie has been linked to some of Hollywood's hottest young stars, from Aaron Carter (a serious fling) to Chad Michael Murray (just a rumor!).

She's learned a thing or two in her dating experience—but she has yet to find her perfect man (even though she just wrapped a movie with that name!). Read on for some of Hilary's top (and most rumored) romances!

32 33

meow!

How did a nice girl like Hilary get caught up in some of Hollywood's Star-Studded Feuds?

40 41

the BIG screen

Take a behind-the-scenes look at Hilary's hit movies

She's played Cinderella, a clumsy student and a modern-day cupid-esque daughter, but Hilary Duff's on-screen roles are just part of the story! Her film career has involved several interesting movies—and even more fascinating facts!

From her first TV movie roles to her most-recent hits, we've got the inside story!

54 55

WHAT HAPPENED TO LIZZIE?

SCREEN SCENE

62

STYLE STAR

Check out some of Hil's top picks!

68 69

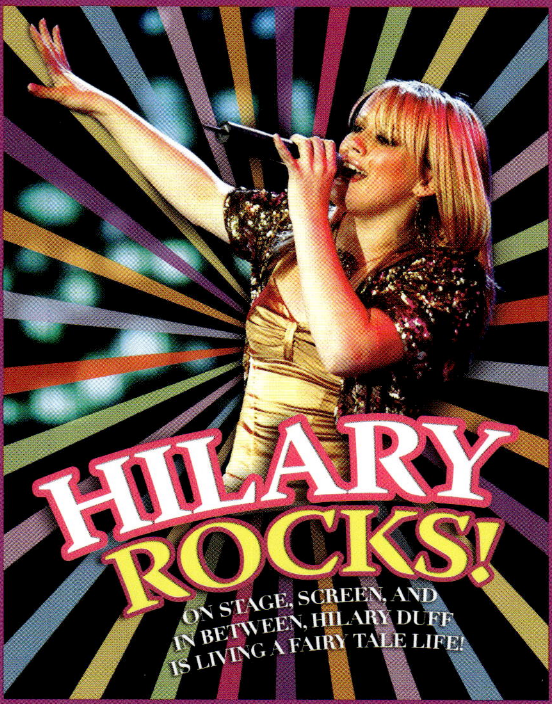

CONTENTS

HILARY ROCKS

04 ROLE OF A LIFETIME
Hilary's newest movie casts her as a modern-day Cinderella; we've got the behind-the-scenes scoop!

10 GROWING UP HILARY
Hilary just bought a house, so is the teen queen "all grown up"?

18 ALMOST FAMOUS
Hilary wasn't always such a star—check out some of her earliest roles to see how they helped shape her career!

24 FAMILY TIES
Hilary's super close with her manager mom and sister, whom she sings with on her new album. The story of how these three are overtaking Hollywood.

32 THE MANY LOVES OF HILARY DUFF
From her bitter breakup with Aaron Carter to her alleged current romance with a 24-year-old rocker, Hilary is a heartbreaker!

40 ME-OW! STAR-STUDDED FEUDS
Hilary and her family have gotten dragged into some nasty word wars with other celebs—you won't believe how and why!

48 SIBLING RIVALRY
The 411 on Haylie Duff, Hilary's super sister.

54 THE BIG SCREEN
Get some popcorn and take a look at Hilary's movie star turns!

62 WHAT HAPPENED TO LIZZIE?
Hilary became famous for her goofy portrayal of teen Lizzie McGuire; why did the series end?

68 STYLE STAR
Hilary's known for her keen fashion sense: a look at her favorite products and clothes.

74 STILL TO COME
A look at what's in store for Hilary in the future!

Written by
Erin Brereton

Development Editor
Bob Baker • Rockett Media

Art Direction
Michael Stassus • Rockett Media

TRIUMPH ENTERTAINMENT
Division of Triumph Books
601 South LaSalle Street
Chicago, Illinois 60605

Role of a Lifetime

Hilary as Cinderella? What a perfect match!

Hilary Duff's wacky, lighthearted *Lizzie McGuire* role made her famous. But even though the 16-year-old made a name for herself playing the girl next door, she was eager to take on a very different role: that of a modern day Cinderella, in *A Cinderella Story.*

After all, her character in the movie, Sam, isn't your average fairy princess in disguise.

"This is really an updated version of the story, and this is probably the most girl-empowered Cinderella we've seen in the movies," Hilary told *Billboard.*

There's more girl power than nervous giggles in *A Cinderella Story.*

"If you look at all the other Cinderella stories, the girl is kind of passive," Duff has said. "Even though it's a great, beautiful story that everyone fell in love with, she doesn't really fight for herself. She kind of waits for things to fall into place and waits for Prince Charming to come and sweep her off of her feet."

"Sam definitely gets support from her friends, but she's very independent, a strong, sensible type of person," Duff said. "Even though she might not be the prettiest girl in school and everyone overlooks her, she still wants to succeed. She's a fighter. Then the guy comes, which is the good perk. But she gets what she wants because she fights for it."

"Even though she might not be the prettiest girl in school and everyone overlooks her, she still wants to succeed," Duff says of her Cinderella character.

Before Midnight

"Cinderella was absolutely my favorite fairy tale growing up," Duff said.

"I think it's every little girl's favorite fairy tale," Duff told reporters. "I was really excited when I got the script and it's all modern-day and updated."

In the film, Hilary plays a quiet, somewhat unpopular teen whose stepmother forces her to work at her late father's diner. But Sam has Ivy League dreams – she wants to attend Princeton. After landing a secret crush in an Internet chat room, the romantic race is on—reminiscent of the original story, but some plot points are updated. There's no glass slipper but there is a cell phone she drops while rushing out of a dance before midnight (after realizing that her crush, who invited her to the dance, is probably out of her league).

The object of her affection, Austin Ames, is played by Chad Michael Murray, 22. Austin is every teenage girl's dream: a high school quarterback who secretly writes poetry and hides his softer side.

Three days into filming, Hilary and co-star Chad Michael Murray, 22, had to shoot their kissing scene. Talk about awkward!

"Hilary had genuine embarrassment," *A Cinderella Story* director Mark Rosman told *Us Weekly*. "You feel it [onscreen]."

In the scene in which they almost kiss, director Mark Rosman told *US Weekly* that "Hilary felt awkward doing it wearing a [mask]." (However, the mask was necessary to conceal her identity.)

Hilary's costumes for the film were equally cumbersome. The princess makeover dress "must have weighed 10 pounds," Hilary has said. "It got annoying," (Still she wore the gown, designed by Monique Lhuillier, to a later charity event.)

The attire wasn't the only challenge during filming. In one scene, Duff takes out some aggression on the baseball field. It wasn't easy for the actress.

"The crew was like, 'You hit like a girl,'" she said. "I'm like, 'I am a girl!'"

A Different Girl

Not only was Hilary homeschooled, but she has always had a tight group of friends—which made her role in *A Cinderella Story* a stretch.

"I don't relate to Sam," Hilary has said. "It's not like I didn't have any friends. So it was cool to have nowhere to pull from and really act."

As always, the actress was up to the challenge.

"I didn't really have much to pull from," Duff said. "I chose this character because our lives are totally different. I've never had a really traumatic thing happen to me or a really hard family life or something. I have had struggles—but not really like her. That's what I wanted,

to try to create a character that isn't like this bubbly happy Hilary, you know? Sam was a little more reserved and a little more introverted."

Mark Rosman is no stranger to Hilary's acting abilities—he directed her in *Lizzie McGuire* and is helming her upcoming film *A Perfect Man.*

"On the first level of this character, there aren't things that Hilary relates to," Rosman told the *Whittier Daily News.* "But anyone can relate to a person with dreams, someone who has something inside them that they're reluctant to express.

"Also, because of her fame, Hilary is an outsider, so to speak. She can't just walk down the street and be a normal person. The character in the film also has difficulty blending in and relating to everyone around her."

"In this movie, Sam really goes all out," Hilary has said. "Even though she's an underdog, gets torn down, bossed around and goes unnoticed, she still has a goal. She's like a fighter — she fights for what she wants and what she believes in — and she gets the guy on top of it."

© Warner Brothers/Courtesy Everett Collection

Other Stars

Hilary's co-stars are a huge part of A Cinderella Story—and she loved working with them!

Jennifer Coolidge, who nabbed laughs in both *Legally Blonde* films, stars as Hil's Botox-obsessed wicked stepmother. Amazingly, Coolidge ad-libbed much of her role (including the killer line "I'm a very appealing person!")

Hilary was a huge fan of Coolidge's zany performance as the self-centered stepmom. "She's such a creative person," she said. "Everybody's been asking, 'What's the most challenging part of the role this time?' and it was biting my cheek trying not to laugh in all of the scenes with her. She's so hilarious and creative, and I loved watching her work. Everything that she did in the movie was hilarious. She ad-libbed a lot of that stuff. She's so funny and interesting to watch."

Hilary's co-stars adored her, too. "Hil rocks," Murray told *Teen People*. "She's so down-to-earth. It's nice to go to work with someone who's not all uptight and who always has a smile on her face."

Regina King plays Hilary's fairy godmother in *A Cinderella Story*. King's 8-year-old son had a huge crush on Hilary (he wrote her love notes during the press junket, to which she responded with a poster autographed "Ian, I like you too.")

"He goes, 'Mom, did you tell Hilary I have a crush on her,' " King told reporters. "I said, 'She knows, Ian. You rapped to her for two weeks when we were on the set. ... Eight- to 12-year-old boys love Hilary Duff. She's like the 'it girl,' and she's so cute and personable, and you see her on *Lizzie McGuire*."

Opening Night

The premiere was July 10, 2004 at Mann's Chinese Theater in Hollywood. And true to the movie's theme, the typical red carpet was cast aside for something a little more princess-like—a lush pink carpet.

Celebs in attendance included

AT A CONCERT IN TAMPA LAST SUMMER, HILARY'S STAGE MANAGER RECEIVED A NOTICE THAT THE PRINCESS OF SAUDI ARABIA WAS AT THE CONCERT BECAUSE SHE IS A HUGE FAN OF HILARY'S! PRINCESS NOUF AND HILARY MET UP AFTER THE SHOW AND CHATTED ABOUT HILARY'S NEW ALBUM!

© Warner Brothers/Courtesy Everett Collection

Heather Locklear, who will play Hilary's mom in the upcoming movie *A Perfect Man*, Jason Ritter, son of the late actor John Ritter and baseball star Jose Conseco.

Audience members reportedly sang along to "Our Lips Are Sealed," Haylie and Hilary's duet, as it played before the movie. After the film was shown, the audience applauded and filed across the street to a club for the afterparty. Once that ended, Hilary headed home to sleep—she had an early flight to Nashville the next morning to rehearse for her summer tour. Never a moment's rest!

Hilary hopes her fans like *A Cinderella Story*—and walk away feeling better about their own high school experience!

"The movie has a lot of life lessons," Duff says. "It's really fun."

GROWING UP HILARY

Hilary just bought a house and nabbed her driver's license—is she all grown up?

In the pack of teen queens currently ruling the cinema, Hilary Duff has staked out some serious space.

Not only has she starred in a string of hit movies—*The Lizzie McGuire Movie* and *A Cinderella Story*, and she has a few more films coming out this year—she has also taken the music industry by storm with her first album, *Metamorphosis.* The record went triple platinum, outselling both Madonna's and Britney Spears' last albums.

In addition, she's launched a line of clothing and accessories this year and is working on a new as-yet-untitled album due for release in fall, 2004.

"I'm excited about my album because it's not characters I'm playing, it's me. It's more personal than acting," Hilary told the *Washington Post*. "The album was so cool to record because all the songs have so much to do with my personal life. I didn't write the songs but I collaborated on all of them. *Metamorphosis* is actually about getting over a boy."

With all that responsibility (and heartache), one might guess Hilary has grown up overnight. But the teen is quick to counter.

"I don't really think about it [my career] too much," she says. "I have a really great team around me that helps me. Of course, sometimes I think, 'Oh well, I should probably do this or that,' but it's really fun for me. Even though I do work my butt off, I still have a good time and try to not make it competitive."

Still, 2004 has been a big year for the teen. In addition to her numerous work projects, she turned 16 and moved into a new house. Check out some of her recent "grown-up" milestones—are they proof that she's all adult now, or just key events in the life of a fun-loving teen?

Hilary Duff

#1: SHE BOUGHT NEW DIGS!

Between touring and filming, Hilary isn't home much—but that didn't stop her from buying a new house. Hilary and her family moved into their new Spanish style mansion in the L.A. area in spring 2004.

And even though she's spent most of the summer traveling, Hilary loves her new home base. "It's the kind of house you don't want to leave!" Hilary told *Us Weekly.*

With six bedrooms, there's plenty of room for Hilary, her 19-year-old sister Haylie, mom (and manager) Susan and dad, Bob, who runs a chain of convenience stores in Texas.

It's just a few blocks from their old L.A. house, but it took the family a year to find the 1920s-era home. Although they've done a lot of redecorating, Hilary says they're nowhere near finished.

"We're not through!" she has said. The Duffs bought the house from a builder, which had its perks. "He left all the pool furniture for us," Hilary said. "Sitting by the pool is very relaxing – it's like being at a resort!"

The large tiled pool is surrounded by white terraces, lush greenery and white pool furniture. The Duffs have decorated the interior of the house using items from several trendy L.A. shops.

Hilary's bedroom is cozy and cute, with its own fireplace, complete with oversized candles on the mantle, rich wooden furniture and plants dotting the room for a homey feel. Her bed is from Arte de Mexico and some accents, including her pillows, came from Heaven on La Brea.

Much of the art in the house was painted by her paternal grandparents. "They were both watercolor painters and we treasure their work," Hilary has said.

The kitchen, which features muted green tones, is the center of the Duff home. "We love the kitchen so we spend a lot of time here," Hilary told *US Weekly* during a recent tour of her new home. "It seems to be our meeting place." Hilary says the family loves to accent the kitchen with fresh cut flowers.

Hilary's favorite dish? "I make a mean grilled cheese!" she says. The family has also been known to cook up a batch or two of cookies in the kitchen. "This is quite a retreat for us!" Hilary has said.

Being a homeowner is a big step toward being an adult, but it hasn't made Hilary lose all sense of childhood whimsy: She was recently spotted blowing a dandelion to make a wish on the Toronto set of her new comedy, The Perfect Man.

#2: SHE GOT HER DRIVER'S LICENSE!

Like most teens, Hilary was anxious to turn 16 and learn to drive.
"Oh my gosh! I've been counting this down for months," she told Girl's Life. And she passed the test with flying colors.

"I got my license and I love to drive all over L.A. I'm such a good driver," she said.

Not that getting her license was a smooth ride. Ashton Kutcher Punk'd Hilary with a fake driving lesson at which her teacher attacked another motorist,

Photo by Lawrence Lucier/FilmMagic.com

© Warner Brothers/courtesy Everett Collection

smashing out his headlights before her purse was stolen by a carjacker!

#3: She's Dealt with Media Gossip

Being a star isn't always easy. When in summer, 2004, several tabloids printed reports that Hilary had put on weight (one even had a weight loss specialist estimate a 15-30 pound weight gain based on a photo taken of Hilary), her publicist shot back saying she hadn't gained a pound and that the photo was just taken from a bad angle.

The press also gleefully reported stories about feuds between stars like Lindsey Lohan and Avril Lavenge, despite Hilary's insistence she had no issues with either celeb.

Her lovelife was also up for grabs. After being photographed with the 25-year-old lead singer of Good Charlotte, Hilary was criticized for dating someone 9 years her senior. She's also been linked to Aaron Carter and her *A Cinderella Story* co-star Chad Michael Murray.

Still, even with all the scrutiny about her alleged boyfriends, Hil's outlook on romance remains positive. "You don't want to put yourself out there to get yourself let down or hurt or something," she told reporters mid-summer. "But I guess if you really care about someone and they really care about you, too, then you sometimes just go for it and let everything go. And have fun with it. It can be exciting."

#4: She's Adjusted to Being Famous

Hilary, who can't go to malls anymore because of the excitement that erupts when she is recognized, is also slowly adjusting to being famous.

"I've tried every kind of disguise but my hair gives me away," she says. "So I tried tucking my hair under a baseball cap and wearing sunglasses but when you see someone wearing a baseball cap and sunglasses, aren't you going to look at them and say, 'Who's hiding under there?'"

Hilary's social life isn't the only thing taking a hit. She's also had encounters with overzealous fans at work-related events.

"One time I was coming out of the premiere of *Cheaper by the Dozen,* the after-party, and there were a lot of people around me like security and stuff because there were such big crowds outside," she says. "And this man came up to me and tried to kiss me."

Her busy schedule has also cut into her free time. The celeb tried to keep a diary but found she was so busy it only lasted for four days.

"I do keep one on my web site so all my fans can see what's going on with me, but you know what? When you're busy, it's really hard," she told the *Washington Post* (in truth, her online diary is filled with apologies for not posting more).

#5: She Headlined a Tour!

Hilary's North American summer concert tour was a huge hit. With more than 30 stops, her "Most Wanted Tour" sold out in several large cities when tickets went on sale.

"Promoters are already asking to add second shows in some markets," Evolution Talent Agency's Craig Bruck, who booked the tour, told the media in July. "Along with Prince and Madonna, Hilary is turning out to be one of the few exceptions to the downturn that has plagued the touring industry this summer."

Others agreed.

"There's a real positive buzz about ticket sales for Hilary's tour," *Pollstar* Editor-in-Chief Gary Bongiovanni said.

But Hilary was more concerned with rocking out than with ticket sales.

"It sounds so cheesy and stupid," she has said. "Words can't really describe how you feel up there and what you get from the crowds of people that are screaming for you and have drawn your name on their clothes and are mouthing the lyrics to all your songs, no matter if they're 4 years old and on their parents' shoulders or a group of 20-year-old college students. It gives you so much energy and makes you feel alive."

She even smoothly handled a show disaster in Atlanta. Six songs into her set, a speaker short-circuited and caught fire, anthe show was stopped for a half hour. (Luckily, no one was hurt!) Hilary, always a trooper, came out and finished the show after the speaker had been fixed!

"This is by far the craziest show ever," she said to the 10,000-person audience.

#6: She's Done Even More Charity Work!

Even with the trials being a celebrity can present, Hilary considers herself very fortunate. Giving back is a huge priority for her—that's why she started working with Kids With a Cause, a nonprofit organization that helps children stricken by poverty, hunger, sickness, a lack of education, abandonment, neglect and/or abuse.

Hilary's been working with Kids With a Cause since it was founded in September 1999, and she is the 2004 Official International Spokesperson. The organization sponsored "Food for a Friend" drives at each of Hilary's summer concerts. Fans were encouraged to bring canned foods to donate to each Hilary show; and the donated food was delivered to shelters in the city where the show was taking place. By mid-summer, the drive had gathered enough food to feed more than 12,000 kids!

Hilary's had quite a busy year—and a busy year before that. Still, those close to the star say she's been careful to maintain her youthful innocence and excitement.

"Oh, she's plenty savvy about this business," *A Cinderella Story* director Mark Rosman says, "but it hasn't turned her into an adult at all. She still laughs at the same things that other 16-year-olds laugh at, and she doesn't get certain things that only adults get. I find that refreshing for someone who's so successful."

Successful, indeed. She spent much of the mid-summer doing TV appearances to promote *A Cinderella Story* and its soundtrack (she performs six of the 14 songs on the album), popping in on ABC's *Good Morning America* (at which her outdoor performance on the show drew a crowd of about 7,000 people), NBC's *The Tonight Show With Jay Leno,* MTV's *Total Request Live, Live With Regis & Kelly* and CBS' *Late Show With David Letterman.*

She may be growing up, but for now, she's still America's top teen. Hilary is well aware her fans watch her every move, but she believes in living her life in a positive, fun way and not obsessing

HILARY ON KEEPING IT COOL IN HOLLYWOOD "I DON'T REALLY THINK ABOUT IT TOO MUCH. I HAVE A REALLY GREAT TEAM AROUND ME THAT HELPS ME. OF COURSE, SOMETIMES I THINK, 'OH WELL, I SHOULD PROBABLY DO THIS OR THAT,' BUT IT'S REALLY FUN FOR ME. EVEN THOUGH I DO WORK MY BUTT OFF, I STILL HAVE A GOOD TIME AND TRY TO NOT MAKE IT COMPETITIVE."

Smallville hunk Tom Welling and Hilary Duff on the set of *Cheaper By the Dozen.*

over all the things—good and bad—that fame has brought her.

"I don't think the role-model thing is a burden," she has said. "Yes, I have to think twice about how I dress when I go out in public because kids are watching me. But I don't stress over it. I don't worry about whether I'm dressing too sexy, too edgy, too trendy or anything like that. I do feel the responsibility, however, and that probably means I won't wear anything too revealing. But I wouldn't anyway. That's not the person I am."

"The burden part is having to deal with the people who want to tear you down. Some people think I'm a joke and I know I shouldn't care what those people think, but it's in my nature to want to make everybody happy. Still, all things considered, the good outweighs the bad."

Singing? Dancing? Acting? Hil does it all!

almost

BEFORE HILARY STARRED AS A MODERN-DAY CINDERELLA, SHE PLAYED A NUMBER OF OTHER CHARACTERS IN TV SHOWS AND MOVIES!

Today, Hilary Duff is one of Hollywood's hottest stars—but it wasn't always that way. For years, she struggled to get noticed in small parts and worked her way up from the small to the big screen. Now that she's taken the entertainment industry by storm with a hit album and several smash movies, it may look like her journey to fame was easy—but the true story of how Hilary became a star is anything but.

star struggles

"When you're a kid, people don't necessarily give you credit for knowing what you want," Hilary has said. "But ever since I was little, even at 6, I knew exactly what I wanted to do and what I wanted to be. I knew I wanted to work, and I knew I was willing to work hard to achieve my goals."

That's why, after doing some commercials at 8, Hilary moved to California with her mother and sister to try to land larger roles. But with her father still in Texas and little luck on the L.A. acting circuit, the Duff girls were soon dejected.

Luckily, their mom, Susan, stepped in to keep the family's spirits high.

"My sister and I must have gone on 100 auditions without a callback," Hilary said, "and the minute my mother saw us

famous

feel like we'd been rejected or this is over, she'd say, 'I don't want to see you guys being upset about this because you weren't right for it.' She would never let us feel like it was our fault."

Hilary's infamous positive attitude also helped.

"I always handled rejection well," she said. "My mom made me believe that it was just a business decision and had nothing to do with me personally."

Eventually, some work trickled in. Hilary landed small roles on *Chicago Hope* and a part in *Casper Meets Wendy.* She also was cast in the pilot of a new NBC sitcom, *Daddio*—but it was dropped before three episodes even aired.

She made her film debut at 10 in an uncredited role in *True Women*, a made-for-TV-movie. She was also in *The Soul Collector,* a 1999 TV movie for which she won a Supporting Actress Young Artist Award.

But before long, work dried up again. Hilary was ready to pack up and move back to Texas when she got the call about auditioning for *Lizzie McGuire.* She didn't want to do it.

"But they sent a plane ticket to come back and audition for it, and I said OK, though I didn't really care about the audition," she says. "I went in and I guess I did a good job."

She won the role and, at 12 years old, began shooting what would become the Disney Channel's highest rated show when it debuted in 2001. The show received 375,000 e-mails a week.

Hilary had arrived, and she soon began taking over the silver screen as well, notably with *Agent Cody Banks* and *The Lizzie McGuire Movie*, which was a hit even as the series ended.

making music

After her single, "I Can't Wait," off the 2002 *Lizzie McGuire* soundtrack went gold, Hilary decided to try her hand at music. Soon came her hit debut album, *Metamorphosis,* which debuted at No. 2 on the *Billboard* charts and quickly climbed to the No. 1 spot.

"Can I tell you how awesome everyone's been to work with?" Hilary said on her web site. "They are the very best writers and producers and musicians ever, and they've been so open to my opinions. It was important to me that all the songs we recorded really meant something special to me

WHAT'S THE HARDEST THING ABOUT BEING HILARY DUFF? "NOT BEING ABLE TO GO OUTSIDE OR GO SHOPPING OR SLEEP IN MY OWN BED AT NIGHT — AND NOT BEING ABLE TO HAVE ANY TIME FOR MYSELF," SHE SAID.

personally. I got to talk with some of the writers and say, 'You know, I feel like this' ... and they really got it, which is so cool. I loved the whole process. It's so exciting. I love that the whole album really relates to me and my life."

Created with the Matrix, a pop songwriting team who has worked with Ricky Martin, Britney Spears, Liz Phair and Avril Lavigne, among others, the album perfectly mirrored Hilary's image—a little bit pop and a little bit punk. "So Yesterday" and "Come Clean" instantly became hits off the album.

But like most other aspects of her career, even releasing an album was a challenge. Few people knew that Hilary had actually once trained professionally as a singer, but given it up to focus on the stage and screen.

"I had taken a couple of singing lessons when I was little, just because I was in a choir," she says. "My sister wanted to do it, so I wanted to do it. And then I just kind of dropped it all because I wanted to be an actress because my sister wanted to act and sing. It was something my sister started out, but I really wanted to do it for my own reasons.

"I've always sung, ever since I could talk," said Hilary. "At home, at school, in the choir, everywhere. But about two years ago I decided to be a real singer, and started working with really cool singers, musicians and songwriters. Best of all, I started working in the studio, experimenting and putting material together. I've really fallen in love with the studio. I just know that a lot of my fans relate to the album."

Still, in show business, street cred is hard to come by, no matter how successful you are.

"People say, 'Oh she's an actress, and now she thinks she's a singer. What a joke!' Or you get people writing horrible reviews about your CD," Hilary told the press. "I really didn't have that much support in the beginning. The radio didn't start playing my music until they started seeing how well my albums sold, and it was really the fans that did that."

The radio finally started playing her songs and eventually helped contribute to the album's huge success. Hilary's new album was released in September; 2004, and she describes it as slightly more edgy, but still accessible.

"I'm so pumped up about (the new album)," she told the *Alameda Times-Star*. "It's so different than the first one. It's much more mature. And I got to write a lot of it and it has more of my opinions, and what I relate to and what I don't, and what needs to be changed."

"But I don't think that it is too mature that kids couldn't listen to it. I just think that other people will relate better."

moving forward

With high school out of the way (Hilary, who was home schooled, finished up and got her GED this year), Hilary is ready to focus full-time on her rapidly expanding career.

As Hilary takes on new acting roles, moves into merchandising with her new Target-exclusive line and takes her music to the stage in her summer tour, she is ready for new challenges.

She may be done for now with formal education but Hilary still views life as a learning experience. "Everybody got along really well, which is great," she said of her summer tour. "And I got to learn so much. I know so much about making a movie and now I got to learn about touring."

And although some say she's overloading on work and missing out on the true teen experience (high school, proms, etc.), Hilary is happy with her lifestyle.

"There have been some sacrifices," she has said. "I know there are big parts of my life that I've probably lost forever, but that's OK. I'm happy.

"If I had to do it all over again, I wouldn't change a thing. I wouldn't trade my life for anyone else's in the world."

photo: John Hayes/Everett Collection)

hil's in the movies

True Women 1997 (TV)
Directed by Karen Arther
Cast Dana Delany, Annabeth Gish, Angelina Jolie, Tina Majorino, Rachael Leigh Cook, Hilary Duff
Based on a book by Janice Woods Windle, this drama centers around how a young girl's life changes after her father dies and she must relocate to Texas to live with her brother-in-law.

Casper Meets Wendy 1998 (TV)
Directed by Bruce McCarthy, Sean McNamara
Cast Billy Burnette, Clay Crosby, Rick Dean, Hilary Duff
Everybody's favorite friendly ghost teams up with Wendy, his witch buddy, to overcome an evil warlock in this sequel to the first Casper film.

The Soul Collector 1999 (TV)
Directed by Michael Scott, Sean McNamara
Cast Bruce Greenwood, Melissa Gilbert, Ossie Davis, Scotty Leavenworth, Todd Allen, Buck Taylor, Hilary Duff
When soul collector Zachariah is sentenced to live on earth for 30 days, he helps out a woman who has just lost her husband (a man Zachariah helped transition to heaven) on her farm.

Lizzie McGuire
2001 (TV series, 2001-2003)
Created by Terri Minsky
Cast Hilary Duff, Adam Lamberg, Taylor Colman, Jake Thomas
Hilary became a star after playing klutzy, daffy Lizzie, who laughs her way through various episodes about growing up (and dealing with embarrassment).

Human Nature 2001
Directed by Michel Gondry
Cast Patricia Arquette, Rhys Ifans, Tim Robbins, Hilary Duff
A scientist and a female naturalist clash over how to study and teach a man they found who was raised in the wild in this comedy about nature versus culture.

Cadet Kelly 2002 (TV)
Directed by Larry Shaw
Cast Hilary Duff, Christy Romano, Gary Cole, Shawn Ashmor, Aimee Garcia
Hilary Duff plays Kelly Collins, a New York teen who finds out that not only is her family moving—they're also sending her to military school.

Agent Cody Banks
2003
Directed by Harald Zwart
Cast Frankie Muniz, Hilary Duff, Angie Harmon, Cynthia Stevenson
In this action-comedy, Cody Banks is a teen working undercover for the CIA who has to befriend a pretty prep school student in order to get close to her father, a scientist developing a fleet of deadly robots.

The Lizzie McGuire Movie
2003
Directed by Jim Fall
Cast Hilary Duff, Adam Lamberg, Hallie Todd, Robert Carradine
After Lizzie McGuire graduates from Junior High, she embarks on a class trip to Rome—and delves headfirst into a romance with a cute Italian singer who whisks her around the city while she plays hooky from school-sponsored events. But it turns out the heartthrob isn't quite who he says he is—which Lizzie discovers just in time to save the day!

Cheaper By The Dozen 2003
Directed by Shawn Levy
Cast Steve Martin, Bonnie Hunt, Tom Welling, Piper Perabo, Hilary Duff, Ashton Kutcher, Missy 'Misdemeanor' Elliott
Based on a real-life story of a family with 12 children, Cheaper By The Dozen features an ensemble cast as a family who relocates from Rhode Island to New Jersey and the hilarity that ensues as they cope with having many, many children.

upcoming parts

Check out some Hilary flicks due out in the next year!

Raise Your Voice
The plot is rumored to involve Hilary playing a small-town girl who heads into the big city (Los Angeles) to spend the summer at a performing arts high school. It's slated for an October, 2004 release.

The Perfect Man
Filmed in Toronto, A Perfect Man stars Heather Locklear as a single mother and Hilary Duff as her teenage daughter who tries to find her mom the perfect mate and ends up in trouble with the law. This film is supposed to be released in spring, 2005.

Outward Blonde
Details are sketchy on this film because it has yet to begin filming, but reportedly it involves a snotty New York teen who flunks gym and is sent to an Outward Bound program.

The Duffs are taking over Hollywood—read all about the Haylie, Hilary and Susan (that's mom!) triple threat!

FAMILY TIES

It may seem unusual that Hilary, who is still under 18 but done with high school, and her sister Haylie, who is 19, still live at home. But with a family as close as the Duffs, it doesn't look like Hilary or Haylie will be moving out of their parents' house anytime soon!

For one, the family just moved into the Spanish-style Los Angeles mansion in spring. But that's not the only reason they're all still calling it home, sweet, home.

Mom Susan, who manages Hilary's career and was a co-producer on *A Cinderella Story*, is extremely close to both her daughters.

In Hollywood, that can be a shelter from the storm. Hilary is still adjusting to being famous—as much as her mom tries to maintain a normal teen experience for her. Hilary has said she can no longer go to malls because she is instantly recognized, and a mom and a manager in the same person provides both guidance and protection.

Case in point: last year someone reportedly broke a basement window in the Duff's home, trying to get in. *The World Entertainment News Network* reported that the next day, Haylie thought she spotted a man who was stalking Hilary parked outside their home. Furious, Susan ran out of the house to confront him and when he peeled away, followed him in a late-night, 50-minute car chase through L.A. with Hilary and Haylie along for the ride.

The man eventually returned home and called the police and said he had been parked in front of their house because of his 16-year-old daughter. However, Susan had another perspective.

"He said he had been at our house because of his 16-year-old daughter. But his daughter wasn't with him," she told

Hilary and Haylie truly are best friends. Despite what different projects and paths their careers take, they are constantly supporting each other.

Photo by S.Sarac/Everett Collection

Photo: John Hayes/Everett Collection

WENN. According to Los Angeles police, the man was investigated and cleared of any wrongdoing.

Still, the family is learning that being famous brings some unwanted attention. But together, they weather it—and prepare to overtake the music and movie worlds!

Sister to Sister

Hilary and Haylie truly are best friends. Despite what different projects and paths their careers take, they are constantly supporting each other. When Hilary began working on her album *Metamorphosis*, Haylie wrote two songs for her sister.

"Since she knows me better than anyone else in the world, Haylie wrote *Sweet Sixteen*, a really fun song that totally relates to my life right now," Hilary said at the time. "She also came up with *Inner Strength* and it's really beautiful. Very empowering and uplifting."

"I write a lot with my sister," Hilary said. "I collaborate with the writers that I work with. I always tell them - and I might not sit down and write a song - but I say, 'This happened to me the other day and I can't get it out of my head and I really think that a song about this would be great,' or 'I think that other people probably deal with this, too.' I also get to sit in on some of the music-making process, and it's really cool."

At the photo shoot for the August *Seventeen* cover featuring Hilary, Haylie tagged along for fun. The sisters read *Us Weekly* during breaks and were excited to spot themselves in an article about celebrity sisters.

"My sister and I are best friends and we get along so well," Duff said. "She is so talented and inspiring to me."

It's a good thing, considering how busy they both are. "We set aside this month for touring, but then in between touring we have to be recording the album on days off, or going to Los Angeles to do press junkets, or... sometimes it gets really crazy, and I just want to drive my car, but I can't, because I really love it," Hilary told *The Oklahomian*. "It's like an addiction where I challenge myself — 'What else can I do?' I'm so lucky I get to do all this stuff right now. Even if I spend some time tired or lonely, it's worth it."

On and By Each Other's Side

The Duff sisters love each other's music ("Hilary called her sister's music "amazing" while different from hers—. "I think her music is more (dance oriented) and mine is more rock"), so much so that they decided to tour together in summer 2004.

Haylie played a six-song set to open each of the shows in Hilary's 2004 summer concert tour. Spending their off days sight-seeing, relaxing, meeting fans and volunteering (they stopped to pass out ice cream at a children's hospital in Greenville, S.C.)., Hilary and Haylie felt like it was a home away from home. "I feel so lucky touring with my sister and having the fans support us," she told the *Salt Lake Tribune*.

Any arguments? No way! Not even when both of them came down with the flu.

"Everybody gets along really well, which is great," Hilary said during the tour.

One of the songs Hilary and Haylie ended their concerts with this summer was "Our Lips are Sealed", a cover they recorded for

Hilary's summer hit *A Cinderella Story.*

"We thought that song worked really well with *Cinderella Story*," Hilary said. "It talks a lot about people talking bad about each other and being popular and being the better person by keeping your lips sealed, I guess."

"We thought that it had a lot to do with my life this past year, all the stuff I went through."

With the recent feuds Hilary has found herself in—with stars such as Lindsay Lohan, Avril Lavinge and others—Haylie has been touchstone. Although, like Hilary, Haylie believes in avoiding trash talk whenever possible, she's always got her sister's back.

When recently rating Lindsay Lohan's outfit for an issue of *Teen People* (which the magazine teased by saying "Will Hilary's big sis trash Lindsay's style? Read on," Haylie took the high road by saying, "She's appropriately perfect all the time," and remarking that Lindsay should lose the bow and massive cleavage on her dress because "she's young and pretty—she doesn't need to do that!"

Perfect answer. But if someone attacks her little sister, watch out!

"Recently when we were on tour, I got a phone call from a certain girl," Hilary told one reporter. "[She] left me a mean message, and I felt really bad. It was something that really was hurtful. I don't know why [she] would do that. Haylie was like totally there for me. She was really sweet about it. We're best friends."

So are their dogs. "I love my dog, Macy," Hilary says. "She's a pocket Pomeranian puppy who's deaf and blind, but still the happiest little thing. Haylie's Pomeranian, Bentley, takes care of her."

Mother Knows Best

Although Susan's been criticized in the past for being a stage mom, Hilary praises her mom for encouraging her to follow her dreams.

"When you're a kid, people don't necessarily give you credit for knowing what you want," Duff has said. "But ever since I was little, even at 6, I knew exactly what I wanted to do and what I wanted to be. I knew I wanted to work, and I knew I was willing to work hard to achieve my goals."

"I just have such a great team around me who knows how to schedule things so there isn't too much interference between all the things I'm working on," Hilary says.

Susan is a tough manager. When Disney stalled on upping Hilary's $15,000-per-episode *Lizzie McGuire* salary, Hilary's representatives—including Susan—urged her to walk. As a result, Hilary severed ties with the show and launched a highly successful music and film career.

But as professional as Susan is, she's still a mom—capable of grounding and of massive embarrassment. When the New *York Daily News* asked about Hilary's childhood nickname, Juicy, her mom started to explain another nickname—to Hilary's protests.

"No way! We are not saying that!" she said. But she finally admitted, "In my family, we have the most crazy nicknames. When my sister was born, she looked like Yoda. So she's Yoda. They call me creature.

Photo by Amy Graves/WireImage.com

AP Photo/Chris Polk, Filmmagic.com

It's kind of a little bit embarrassing. I can't believe the whole world knows this now."

Mark Rosman, who directed Hilary in *Lizzie McGuire* and *A Cinderella Story*, says Susan has helped keep Hilary a normal, down-to-earth teen.

"I always handled rejection well," Duff said. "My mom made me believe that it was just a business decision and had nothing to do with me personally."

When Hilary, Haylie and Susan first moved to Los Angeles when Hilary was 10, their father remained in Houston, where he runs a business, visiting L.A. every three or so weeks.

Since Hilary's career has taken off, her mom has gotten into producing—she was involved with *A Cinderella Story* and *A Perfect Man* and will undoubtedly work behind the scenes on future Hilary projects.

But she still finds time to be Hilary's mom—not just her manager. When Hilary was in Toronto recently filming *Raise Your Voice* with Rita Wilson and John Corbett, Susan cooked dinner for her every night.

"We'd eat our supper in front of the TV set watching *Fear Factor*," Hilary told the *London Free Press*. "People were eating all these horrible bugs and things and it still didn't turn me off my food."

Hilary's mom also works to make sure her daughter's life is as close to a normal teen experience as it can be. When Hilary, who was home schooled, lamented not having gone to a prom, she convinced actor Dan Byrd, who plays her best friend in *A Cinderella Story*, to throw an '80s prom party in his new apartment before his furniture arrived.

"I kept saying how much I missed not having a prom, so all my best friends and I threw our own impromptu one," Hilary told the *London Free Press*.

She and her friends bought vintage prom dresses from local thrift stores and she wore plastic pumps and big hair. As for the prom snacks? Enter Susan, mom extraordinaire.

"We decorated the apartment with streamers and everything," Hilary said. "My mom made finger food and we had this big punch bowl and there was a photographer and everything. There were about 50 people."

To Hilary, who once said her first stop after getting her driver's license would be "to get my mom's breakfast." Susan is the perfect mom—and she's enabled Hilary to have the perfect career.

"I'm really lucky to have gotten to do so many things at such a young age," Hilary told MTV. "Hopefully, I can just keep doing it."

"IN MY FAMILY, WE HAVE THE MOST CRAZY NICKNAMES. WHEN MY SISTER WAS BORN, SHE LOOKED LIKE YODA. SO SHE'S YODA. THEY CALL ME CREATURE. IT'S KIND OF A LITTLE BIT EMBARRASSING."

the many loves of Hilary Duff

Hil's love life is almost as hectic as her filming schedule!

Hilary Duff has already achieved fame (she's made hit songs and hit movies!) and fortune (how many other teens do you know who've bought a mansion?) – now she's got one more horizon to conquer: boys!

Not that Hilary hasn't been logging in some serious guy time. The 16-year-old cutie has been linked to some of Hollywood's hottest young stars, from Aaron Carter (a serious fling) to Chad Michael Murray (just a rumor!).

She's learned a thing or two in her dating experience—but she has yet to find her perfect man (even though she just wrapped a movie with that name!). Read on for some of Hilary's top (and most rumored) romances!

Photo by Jon Kopaloff/FilmMagic.com

DID YOU KNOW HILARY WANTED TO ACT EVEN AS A YOUNG KID? "I JUST HAD THIS CRAZY DRIVE TO WORK," SHE SAID. "I STARTED DOING COMMERCIALS AND MODELING. THAT WAS PRETTY MUCH ALL YOU COULD DO IN TEXAS. I WAS BEGGING TO COME OUT TO CALIFORNIA AND TRY THIS OUT."

Aaron Carter

Hilary may deny most of the dating rumors that surround her, but she's gone on the record about her relationship with Aaron Carter—at least, somewhat.

Fans were often confused about whether or not Aaron and Hilary were an item—but chances are that was because Aaron and Hilary were often confused, too.

When Aaron showed up at *The Lizzie McGuire Movie* premiere with Hilary, even he wasn't sure of their status. "I turned up today because Hilary told me she'd tell me what's going on with us," he told reporters. (He then told them to ask Hilary whether or not they were dating).

"We have to be so careful because we're teenagers and stuff happens, like breaking up and getting back together," Hilary told *Girl's Life.* "It's like any normal teenage relationship. Aaron is such a cool guy. He makes me laugh."

Some days, it seemed pretty clear. Aaron is said to be the source of Hilary's much-publicized feud with Lindsay Lohan. Rumor has it that Hilary showed up with Aaron in tow to shoot a *Vanity Fair* cover that featured several teen stars—and allegedly those celebs were none too happy to see Aaron.

Since some of the actresses (including Lindsay, who was at the shoot) had dated Aaron, things were tense. "It was really uncomfortable when he walked in," an unnamed source said about the incident.

Aaron's certainly made a name for himself around Hollywood's teen dating scene. The younger brother of Backstreet Boy Nick Carter, Aaron shot to popularity with his *Aaron's Party* CD and won the Nickelodeon Kids Choice Award for Favorite Rising Star and the Teen Choice Award for Choice Male Artist of the Year in 2001.

The two rising stars seemed to be the perfect couple; but their busy schedules proved to be a problem.

"I just want to say one thing: Me and Aaron, OK ... It's cool when he comes to L.A. because we get to see each other," Hilary told *Girl's Life* while they were dating. And when they couldn't get together? Things weren't as easy.

Happy couple Hilary and Aaron Carter from back during the *Lizzie McGuire Movie* premiere

Photo by Lester Cohen/WireImage.com

Hilary and Aaron allegedly broke up because having a long-distance relationship was too hard, and the stars were traveling too much to further their careers. Hilary claims they're still good friends.

"It was too hard to be in a relationship when you're working, and my mind's somewhere else and we're always away from each other," she said.

Aaron is now dating Brooke Hogan, daughter of professional wrestler Hulk Hogan.

Joel Madden

Rumors started swirling after Hilary was photographed hanging out with Good Charlotte singer Joel Madden in Toronto, where she was filming *The Perfect Man*.

Photo by Gregg DeGuire/WireImage.com

Reports of sightings started flooding in: Hilary and Joel having a romantic dinner at Morton's steakhouse in June, 2004 in Toronto and later kissing outside the restaurant; Joel stopping during a walk the same month to peck her on the cheek several times; and, the couple spending some quality time at the Much Music Video Awards in Canada.

At the awards, a reporter asked Joel if he and Hils were dating and Joel reportedly just smiled and walked away.

Then, in late June, 2004, the couple was said to be cuddling at a party thrown by *Maxim* magazine.

Why all the secrecy? Well, Hilary's just 16—and Joel is 25, so some have speculated they it might look badly that Hilary is dating an older man. Others just thought she was being secretive because of how burned she was when her relationship (and subsequent breakup) with Aaron was played out in the media.

Or there might be another reason – they're not dating. Hilary's rep said the two are just friends. Joel reportedly said in a recent interview that he doesn't have a girlfriend. Still, the frequent sightings of the twosome have left many to wonder ... will Joel be Hilary's next boyfriend? Not according to Hilary ...

"I can't have a boyfriend right now," she says. "And I'm definitely not interested in him. I think his band is cool, and we're friends, but we walk down the street together one time and all of a sudden we're like a couple."

Photo by Lee Celano/WireImage.com

Hilary met Jordan Masterson while filming *Cheaper By the Dozen*, but the two have since parted ways after a short but friendly romance.

Jordan Masterson

When Hilary started filming *Cheaper By the Dozen*, she knew she'd be making a great movie—but she didn't know she'd pick up a boyfriend along the way.

Yet she did. Although she met Jordan Masterson on the set of the film, they didn't hook up until a year later when they bumped into each other at an event in Encino, Calif.

The Duff clan digs 17-year-old Jordan.

"I couldn't be happier. Jordan's a great kid and he's an actor, so he understands," Haylie told Net Music Countdown.

Jordan, whose brother Danny Masterson is on That '70's Show, has appeared on a number of TV shows, such as *The George Lopez Show, Malcolm in the Middle* and *Grounded for Life*.

"He's so nice. I love him," Hilary said of her then current boyfriend.

So what happened? After several months of dating, their busy careers took a toll on the couple – and in April, Hilary announced on a U.K. TV show that she and Jordan had called it quits. But the couple remains friends.

Photo by Stephen Lovekin/FilmMagic.com

Lessons Learned

Haylie Duff told the press she's learned from Hilary's rocky love life.

"I think family questions are OK, but I don't plan on ever talking about my relationships," she said. "After all that happened with Hilary and Aaron Carter, I've learned it's best not to even go there. They weren't even dating for that long and people made it into so much more than it even was."

Hilary has learned a thing or two, as well. "I'm kind of like Sam in a way," she said, referring to her character in *A Cinderella Story*. "I'm cautious and I don't want to put myself out there to let myself down or get hurt."

Hilary tends to go for low-key guys. "I don't really like guys who look like they spend more time in front of the mirror than I do," she said. "And they have to be smart."

Despite being cautious in romance, Hilary certainly has her share of male admirers – to her constant surprise.

"I'm such a normal person and I'm like, 'Why is it people feel like this toward me?' " she said. "It's a very good feeling, and it's very sweet and very thoughtful. I get letters all the time - and flowers and gifts. It's very flattering, and it's kind of surreal."

other loves

Of course, Hilary's not one to gossip—which is why it's so hard to determine exactly who she's dating. Check out these rumors!

• Frankie Muniz – after starring with Frankie in the first *Cody Banks* film, some fans thought she had struck up a real life romance with the *Malcolm in the Middle* star. But the truth is, Hils and Frankie are just good friends-such good friends she has said it was sort of awkward to kiss him in the film!

• Chad Michael Murray – after Hilary and Chad, 22, showed up at the *Freaky Friday* premiere holding hands, the rumor mill went into high gear. Maybe their performance in *A Cinderella Story* seemed a little too real ...when *USA Today* questioned *A Cinderella Story* director Mark Rosman about a possible romance between the two stars, even he replied with a terse, "You'll have to ask them."

• Prince Harry – Holy highness! Rumor has it British royal Prince Harry (brother of William, son of Charles and Diana) became intrigued with Hilary after seeing T*he Lizzie McGuire Movie*. A source told the *Daily Star* in February that Harry initiated contact and the two chatted on the phone last February. So is it true? Hils isn't talking—but don't forget, similar rumors have floated around about the royals and Britney Spears and Christina Aguilera!

The bottom line? They're totally just friends. In fact, Chad is engaged to his One Tree Hill costar Sophia Bush, who came with him to the *A Cinderella Story* premiere. "It would be a huge scandal," Duff laughed about the romance rumors.

Chad Michael Murray
and Hilary Duff
Visit MTV's "TRL"

Photo by Gregg DeGuire/WireImage.com

me

HOW DID A NICE GIRL LIKE HILARY GET CAUGHT UP

Photo by Kevin Mazur/WireImage.com

First Lindsay. Then Avril. It seemed like last year everyone had something not-so-nice to say about poor Hilary. And just when it looked like it couldn't get any worse, suddenly people were calling out her mom and sister!

Hilary's not one to pick fights, but somehow she ended up in a few recently. Take a look at some of Hil's most recent battles.

OW!

IN SOME OF HOLLYWOOD'S STAR-STUDDED FEUDS?

Avril vs. Hilary

Avril Lavigne may or may not have meant to say that seeing her fans dressing like Avril made her mad, but someone told Hilary she did—and Hilary responded by criticizing Avril for lashing out at her fans.

Avril's response? You guessed it – criticizing Hils.

"They quoted Hilary Duff saying, 'Avril needs to appreciate her fans more and blah, blah, blah, blah,'" Lavigne told *Newsweek*. "I'm like, excuse me? First off, it's not even true. I never said that. And second, who the hell cares what she has to say about my fans? Whatever. Hilary Duff's such a goody-goody, such a mommy's girl."

Avril then admitted she'd never met Hilary and sarcastically suggested she was "sure she's really nice and really sweet. I'm sure she's all smiles."

True to form, Hilary had nothing but nice things to say about her alleged feud with Avril.

"I've never really ever actually met her in real life," Hilary said. "I see her all the time at events, and you know what? I think that I'm a pretty nice person, and I said something one time that wasn't very nice. It wasn't like I meant it to be mean, but I saw this thing where she said, `I don't want my fans to dress like me. Find your own style.' I was like, `Well, you know, people should embrace their fans looking up to you instead of pushing them away.'"

"That's what I said, and I think that she took it the wrong way. I apologized and I'm sorry."

When another publication asked her about her word war with Avril Lavigne, Hilary downplayed the feud.

"With Avril Lavigne, her CD is in my car right now," she said. "You know what I did? I said something I shouldn't have said. I said she should respect her fans more. And then she called me a mommy's girl or a good girl. I don't care. I am a good girl."

Lindsay vs. Hilary

The rivalry between Lindsay Lohan and Hilary Duff runs deep. For one, they're both two of the hottest young actresses in Hollywood, often vying for similar roles and battling at the box office with new movies. Secondly, they run in some of the same circles. For example, Lindsay starred with Chad Michael Murray in *Freaky Friday* and is reportedly friendly with the actor. Hilary co-starred with him in *A Cinderella Story* and has been spotted out on the town with him.

But the conflict between the *Mean Girls* and *Freaky Friday* star and the *A Cinderella Story* celeb allegedly began over a boy: pop star Aaron Carter.

Both girls dated Carter at one time—who dated him first is a matter of opinion. Supposedly, Hilary dated him first—then the two broke up, and he dated Lindsay—and then they broke up, and he started dating Hilary again.

The feud escalated when Duff arrived at the premiere for *Freaky Friday*, which starred Lindsay, with Aaron, Lindsay's ex-boyfriend.

Photo by Gregg DeGuire/WireImage.com

AP Photo/Nam Y. Huh)

Tension between the two continued to mount when Hilary allegedly tried to have Lindsay thrown out of the *Cheaper by the Dozen* premiere (a film starring Hilary).

Anyone's head spinning? So was Hilary's!

"Honestly? I couldn't even tell you [why all these fights have broken out]," she said. "With Lindsay Lohan, I don't think she likes me very much."

"She's made a big deal out of nothing," Hils said. "I guess she really got angry with that."

Hilary says she has only met Lindsay three times.

"She has a really big problem with me," Hilary said. "She kept saying all these rumors about me, like I manhandled her. I think that I'm a very positive person. I was really upset when she was saying these things about me. I don't know her. I think she's really talented."

The rumors upset her, but Hilary tried to remain upbeat about all the negative press that erupted during the feud.

"People are going to say what they're going to say, and you can't make everybody happy," she said. "I do have a thick skin, and I'm a pretty strong person. You just can't let that stuff get to you. And usually people who make comments about people they don't like are insecure, and it makes them feel better."

Much of the negative press around the feud seemed to focus on Lindsay. In fact, she came under fire when she described her battle with Hilary as "retarded" in interviews. Her use of the word "retarded" prompted The Arc, a national organization for people with mental retardation, to write her a letter requesting she stop using the word "retarded". (Lohan had also referred to rumors of her getting breast implants and a paparazzi incident as "retarded" as well.)

To her credit, when asked about the fight by reporters, Lindsay had nothing but nice things to say about Hilary.

"Maybe she has a problem with me, but I don't think she should," Lindsay said. "She doesn't need that. Her career is going great."

The *Freaky Friday* star also stressed that the argument had been blown out of proportion.

"I read recently that I had a dartboard of Hilary in my apartment!" she told one magazine. "Why would I take the time to put up a photo on a dartboard of someone I am cool with? It's just silly stuff."

DURING ONE TRL APPEARANCE BROUGHT 4,000 HILARY FANS OUT ON THE STREET! (THE AREA AROUND MTV'S STUDIO HAD TO BE SHUT DOWN). A CINDERELLA STORY GROSSED $30 MILLION IN LESS THAN TWO WEEKS.

Ashlee vs. Hilary

Even seemingly friendly Simpson sister Ashlee is taking digs at poor Hilary! *Us Weekly* reported that Ashlee, younger sister of Newlyweds star Jessica Simpson, criticized Hilary's music while recording her own debut album. Sure, it was probably just a comment (Ashlee also railed against her sister's brand of positive pop)—but the last thing Hilary needs is another famous feud!

Paris vs. Haylie

Paris Hilton is no stranger to bad press—after first being labeled an over-the-top party girl, she was at the center of a scandal in 2003. So why is she taking on poor Haylie?

Apparently, Paris—who is also preparing her debut album, reportedly called *Paris is Burning*—recorded one of the same tunes Haylie recorded for her album (the song was a little ditty called "Screwed"). Paris had previously announced that "Screwed" wold be the first single off her album, which will be released on her new Heiress label

Instead, Haylie won the rights to the song.

The Media vs. Hil's Mom

Even Hilary and Haylie's mom has come under fire! Their mother, Susan, is closely involved in both girls' careers (she's been Hilary's manager for ages), and as a result, she's gotten some

HILARY'S

HILARY'S FAN CLUB

Not all celebs have problems with Hilary! Check out what some famous Hilary fans had to say about the teen queen:

"SHE IS COMPLETELY JUST A LIGHT TO THE WORLD. SHE IS SO BEAUTIFUL AND SO INCREDIBLY SWEET. ... I'M A BIG FAN OF HERS! SHE IS JUST A DOLL ... AND HER PERSONALITY IS AMAZING SO I DON'T THINK SHE NEEDS ADVICE. MAYBE, IF ANYTHING, JUST BE HERSELF AND NEVER CHANGE!"
— BRITNEY SPEARS

"WHEN YOU WORK WITH KIDS, YOU NORMALLY GET A CANNED, PROCESSED KID-ACTING QUALITY, BUT SHE WAS NATURAL, SWEET AND GENUINELY OPTIMISTIC."
— MARK ROSMAN, *LIZZIE MCGUIRE* AND *A CINDERELLA STORY* DIRECTOR

FAN CLUB

"SHE'S A REALLY TALENTED ACTRESS. SHE'S REALLY SPONTANEOUS AND SHE REALLY ACTS IN THE MOMENT, SO SHE KEEPS EVERY SCENE REALLY FRESH AND ALIVE. SHE BRINGS SO MUCH ENERGY AND SPONTANEITY AND LIFE TO THE THINGS SHE DOES THAT IT REALLY MAKES YOUR JOB A LOT EASIER BECAUSE THE CHEMISTRY WAS JUST THERE!"
— YANI GELLMAN, FROM *THE LIZZIE MCGUIRE MOVIE*

"KEEP DOING WHAT YOU'RE DOING. YOU MUST BE DOING SOMETHING RIGHT BECAUSE MY SISTERS HAVE YOUR ALBUM. THEY LISTEN TO IT 24/7. THAT'S ALL I HEAR ALL DAY!"
— LIL ROMEO

"SHE'S LIKE THE 'IT GIRL,' AND SHE'S SO CUTE AND PERSONABLE."
— REGINA KING

negative press about being a too-controlling presence and a stage mom.

When recently asked whether or not the rumors were true, Hilary strongly defended her mom. (They're super close!)

"I love my mom," she said. "I totally look up to her, and she just doesn't let anybody take advantage of me. People might call that a stage mom."

Keeping it Real

Hilary is well aware that negative press—as well as positive press–is part of being a celebrity.

"Just because I have a movie coming out or [someone] has an awesome album or single, it's like everyone turns it into this huge thing that's so stupid."

"The burden part is having to deal with the people who want to tear you down," Hilary has said. "Some people think I'm a joke and I know I shouldn't care what those people think, but it's in my nature to want to make everybody happy. Still, all things considered, the good outweighs the bad."

And at the end of the day, Hilary stays positive with a little help—from her fans.

"I think that it's really great that people love me and that people hate me," she said. "I see it all the time. That's great. It's really great that people have their opinions about things. Sometimes I think that people can be a little mean-spirited, and why waste your energy being like that? Personally, I don't choose to hate people. But if people are opinionated, like a lot of people hate my music, well, a lot of people love my music."

SIBLING RIVALRY?

After touring with her sister, Haylie Duff is getting almost as much attention as Hilary—but are they competing? No way!

Hilary Duff may be the biggest star in the Duff family—but, according to Hilary, her 19-year-old big sister Haylie had the idea first.

"I had taken a couple of singing lessons when I was little, just because I was in a choir," says Hilary. "My sister wanted to do it, so I wanted to do it. And then I just kind of dropped it all because I wanted to be an actress because my sister wanted to act and sing. It was something my sister started out, but I really wanted to do it for my own reasons."

Now, the Duff sisters—both getting more famous by the minute—are a rare Hollywood pair: super-close and not at all competitive. Honestly. Not even a little.

"My sister and I are best friends and we get along so well," Duff has said. "She is so talented and inspiring to me. She's my role model."

Not only do both girls still live together (with their parents), they support each other's careers and ambitions. Their genuine affection has deep roots in their Texas upbringing.

"We grew up in San Antonio," Hilary said. "We grew up in the hill country. We didn't really have anyone else around. We only had each other to play with and I think that's why we are so close. We share everything. She's awesome."

Hilary Hits First

Although both sisters moved to Los Angeles with their mother at the same time and started pounding the pavement for roles, they had mixed success. Hilary has attributed Haylie's landing a commercial as a key motivating factor

Photo by Steve Granitz/WireImage.com

for the family staying and sticking it out when the roles were few and far between; but before long, it was Hilary who was getting more parts.

When she landed her starring role in the hit *Lizzie McGuire* sitcom and starred in a string of hit movies (*Agent Cody Banks, The Lizzie McGuire Movie,* and *Cheaper By The Dozen* to name a few), it seemed that one sister would be left behind in the dust.

However, Hilary refused to let that happen. Not only is her sister a frequent companion when she is out and about—Haylie attended one of Hilary's autograph signings at the Virgin Megastore in New York City, she went with Hilary to the *2003 MTV Movie Awards*, and the two have even been know to hit the L.A. scene in matching Mickey T-shirts—she also recently dueted with Hilary on a song for the *A Cinderella Story* soundtrack. They belted out a remake of the GoGo's hit "Our Lips Are Sealed" for the movie.

"We love working together," Hilary told Billboard. "We decided to do a version of 'Our Lips Our Sealed' because it's a good message for stuff that's going on in the movie and in my life, like dealing with gossip and all that high school drama."

Turns out the song is an old favorite in the Duff household.

"Our favorite movie is *Romy and Michelle's High School Reunion* and 'Our Lips Are Sealed' is in it," Hilary says. "We've said before, 'Oh, my God, we have to do that song,' and when we recorded it together and did the video for it, we had a blast"

Haylie thought so, too. "Filming our video was one of our favorite experiences," she recently told *M* magazine. "We were just talking about how lucky we were that we got to do something like that together. I seriously don't know anybody else who gets along with their sister as well as I do. We just had the best time!"

The song has continued to climb the charts and is helping Haylie become known as more than just "Hilary Duff's big sister." The two also acted together in an episode of *American Dreams*—they appeared as the '60s group the Shangri-Las and sang one of the group's hits. They also hosted the Gillette Venus Divine "Legs of a Goddess" contest in New York's Times Square, a nationwide search to find the woman with the best legs in America.

HILARY STARRED AS A BALLERINA IN A PRODUCTION OF THE NUTCRACKER WHEN SHE WAS IN GRADE SCHOOL.

HILARY HAS SAID THAT SHE AND HAYLIE WENT ON 100 AUDITIONS WITHOUT LANDING A ROLE WHEN THEY FIRST CAME TO HOLLYWOOD.

© S. Sarac/Everett Collection

Hil and Haylie hold hands while singing "We Got the Beat" on the *Good Morning America Show*.

Screen Queen

An accomplished actress in her own right, Haylie has appeared in a number of films, including *The Addams Family Reunion*, *I Love Your Work* and *True Women* (which Hilary also appeared in!).

Haylie surprised many moviegoers by appearing in the indie film, *Napoleon Dynamite,* earlier this year. In the movie, she played a snobby mean girl.

"She is just a really nasty, mean girl," Haylie told MTV News "She's part of the Happy Hands Club, a sign-language club where we learn, like, Backstreet Boys songs. I end up running [for class president] against this unpopular kid who doesn't stand a chance at winning."

The role was not just a stretch from her own personality, but the complete opposite of what people were used to seeing a Duff play on screen.

Viewers took notice. But when one reporter asked Haylie if she chose to play a nasty girl to contrast Hilary's many good girl roles, she scoffed at the idea.

"We never planned it that way," Haylie told *M* magazine. "I just loved the script. And it's nice to play someone who is the opposite of yourself. Hilary will eventually play a mean girl, too!"

And, as always, Hilary was first in line to support her sister, mentioning her work whenever possible. "Haylie's an amazing performer," she said to one reporter who asked about their relationship, "Have you seen her in '*Napoleon Dynamite*'?"

Photo by Jason Merritt/FilmMagic.com

Haylie's next role is in a film called *Crazy House*, due to be released next year.

"There's a lot of funny parts, but it's actually a horror film," she says. "We get trapped in this crazy house, but you find out at the end it's a really funny joke. But it's really scary. I get to choreograph a knife fight. This lady tries to kill me with a knife."

Stage Sisters

With the success of their "Our Lips Are Sealed" duet, there was only one more thing to do: Take this show on the road. When Haylie opened for Hilary on her summer tour, Hilary felt her fans were more than willing to accept her big sis.

"I think people have always been wondering about her and what's she's about. She has great music and she writes all of it. I love being on tour with her. We have a blast," she told the media.

Haylie was also psyched about hitting the road—because of the show and because of the potential sibling bonding experiences that could occur.

"I'm so excited about the tour!" she said. "I haven't gotten to spend much time with Hilary recently. The show is not super choreographed. I'll be doing some dancing, and my sister is like a total rocker chick! But we've got some cool surprises."

Perhaps the coolest surprise of all was being able to spend weeks traveling and not have it feel chaotic.

"I'm having so much fun," told the *Alameda Times-Star* partway through her tour. "I get to tour with my sister, which makes it even better and makes it feel more like home, and we have two of the dogs with us and two of my friends."

HAYLIE ROCKS OUT

So what's next from Haylie? The singer is about to release her debut album.

"As far as my musical style, it's a lot of everything," she says. "There's some acoustic stuff, but then there's some old-school Courtney Love-sounding stuff. I don't want my album to be just one style."

A talented musician, Haylie wrote one song—"Inner Strength"—for Hilary's *Metamorphosis* album. She also co-wrote another song, "Sweet Sixteen," for the record.

The songs for Haylie's upcoming album will differ from those she penned for her sister.

"When I'm writing for myself I don't censor myself as much, just because I'm a little bit older," Haylie told MTV News, "so I can say some things she can't and be a little edgier."

Haylie has described her soon-to-be-released record as techno-esque. It's another difference from Hilary, who has said too much techno gives her a headache.

"It's a high energy dance album that you can listen to while you're getting ready to go out," Haylie says of her upcoming release. "It'll be out in mid-August. My first single is 'Screwed.'"

The single garnered national media attention in late summer when Paris Hilton announced she, too, planned to release the song "Screwed" as the first single off her debut album.

Allegedly the situation has been sorted out and several sources have reported Haylie will release the song first.

"It's about a girl who loves the guy, but he doesn't care about her. So she's like, 'Since I'm already screwed, I'm just going to tell you how I feel,'" Haylie says.

Screwed is one thing Haylie's never felt—although many sisters in her place might have — always in the shadow of a younger, more famous sister, it can't be easy. But although Haylie sometimes stresses their differences, she is quick to say they are as close as can be.

The sisters are each others' biggest fans, when talking to the media about their newest projects or when privately addressing each other's contributions, such as Hilary's *Metamorphosis* liner notes, in which she thanked Haylie for being the "best role model" and told her she loved her.

"It's not that I didn't want to be seen as Hilary's sister, because I'm very proud to be her sister," Haylie said on 20/20. "I know how talented she is and I know that I'm talented too. And I never wanted it to look like we used her talent to get me to where I wanted to be."

The Big Screen

Take a behind-the-scenes look at Hilary's hit movies

She's played Cinderella, a clumsy student and a modern-day cupid-esque daughter, but Hilary Duff's on-screen roles are just part of the story! Her film career has involved several interesting movies—and even more fascinating facts!

From her first TV movie roles to her most-recent hits, we've got the inside story!

Although the critics did not buy into Hil's version of Cinderella, her fans loved it which is good enough for her

Photo by George Pimentel/WireImage.com

True Women

Hils made her film debut in this 1997 TV movie, which was filmed in her home state of Texas. For Hilary, whose family has lived in Texas for generations, the plot—involving a girl moving to Texas to live with family after her father dies—must've held some geographical significance for the young star!

Casper Meets Wendy

A sequel to the 1995 film Casper starring Christina Ricci, *Casper Meets Wendy* starred Hilary as Wendy, Casper's red-hooded friend. It was released on video in September 1998 in the United States.

Still new to film roles, Hilary found the challenges of making *Casper Meets Wendy* daunting at times—but hysterical.

"On the set of *Casper Meets Wendy*, I was chasing after a goat for this one scene," she says. "The director screamed at me, 'Meaner, meaner!' I ran faster with this angry expression on my face."

"[Then] the director yelled cut. 'Hilary, what are you doing?' he said. I told him I was just following directions. Turns out he was calling the goat—his name was Meaner."

The Soul Collector

Hilary starred as Ellie in this 1999 TV movie, which also filmed in Texas (in Austin and Bastrop, Texas). In the film, a soul collector must live on earth for a month and help a widow with maintaining her farm.

Human Nature

Written by zany screenwriter Charlie Kaufman (who also penned *Being John Malkovich* and *Adaptation*), Hilary appeared as a younger version of Patricia Arquette's character, Lila Jute. The 2001 film, a humorous take on a found man who was raised in nature, was directed by Michel Gondry, who also directed singer Bjork's trippy *Human Behavior* video. (In fact, many of the forest scenes in *Human Nature* are said to be allusions to that video!)

Cadet Kelly

Hilary starred as Kelly Collins, a New York teen sent to military school who struggles to fit in among the army-minded. Filmed in Toronto, this 2002 flick had a Macy Gray song on its soundtrack.

Agent Cody Banks

In 2003, Hilary tackled the role of a scientist's daughter whom Agent Cody Banks, played by Frankie Muniz, must get close to in order to stop Hil's film dad from developing a fleet of deadly robots.

The clever comedy was a huge hit with fans, partially because of its plot and partially because of its attention to cinematic detail. (Such as the prep school Cody and Natalie attend, the William Donovan Preparatory School. William Donovan was in charge of the U.S. Office of Strategic Services in World War II, which eventually became the CIA!)

Hilary found the role was surprisingly similar to her TV alter ego, Lizzie McGuire.

"Lizzie McGuire was really into makeup and hair and clothes and whatever the style was," she said. "Same with Natalie in *Agent Cody Banks*. She was a very popular girl at school and she had everything going for her."

The film also starred a number of talented adult actors, such as Angie Harmon, formerly of *Law and Order*, and Darrell Hammond from *Saturday Night Live.*

The Lizzie McGuire Movie

Following up her co-starring role in *Agent Cody Banks*, Hilary launched headfirst into her own movie—the big screen finale of her hit Disney series. *The Lizzie McGuire Movie* featured Lizzie and crew on a class trip to Rome—during which Lizzie is swept off her feet by a hot Italian teen singing star. (Which was, of course, a great excuse to work Hilary singing into the plot!)

Filmed in Los Angeles, Vancouver and Rome, *The Lizzie McGuire Movie* was a hit with fans, making a profit that was more than twice what the film cost to make.

Even though some creative license was taken with various plot points and Italian locations (the awards show at the end of the film allegedly takes place in the Roman Coliseum, despite the fact only part of the floor at the real Coliseum is covered by a sandy wooden deck and there is only seating for 700 people—and people haven't been allowed in the top of it for 1,500 years!), the movie is a fun, funny end to the much-loved *Lizzie McGuire* series.

But the movie wasn't the only Lizzie success story—the soundtrack to the film contained Hilary's hit song, "Why Not"—a double treat for Hilary and Lizzie fans!

Cheaper By the Dozen

Even though the names, gender ratio and most other details about the 12 children in the original *Cheaper By The Dozen* book were changed for the 2003 film, it stood to reason this new film version would feature an all-star cast to attract audiences.

But who could imagine Hilary Duff, Ashton Kutcher and Tom Welling (the hottie from Smallville) all in one movie?

Apparently some producers could—because all three of the young celebs are in *Cheaper By the Dozen* – the story of a family who relocates from Rhode Island to New Jersey.

Hilary says *Cheaper By the Dozen* dad, Steve Martin, kept the cast in stitches.

The movie was a gigantic hit—it earned $27.6 million in its first three days and eventually reaped in $163.4 million worldwide! In addition, 3 million DVD and VHS copies were bought on the first day of the movie's home video release, according to Fox Home Video.

But Hilary wasn't thinking about cash when she signed on to make *Cheaper By The Dozen.* She was thinking about how much fun the movie would be to make! Hilary had nothing but nice things to say about her co-stars. Steve Martin, who plays the dad in *Cheaper By The Dozen*, kept the cast in stitches. ("He's so funny!" Hilary said of the comedian).

And Ashton's hunky looks didn't go unnoticed, either. Her comment on Demi Moore's main man? "He's so cute!" (Ashton once Punk'd Hilary with a fave driving lesson; his *Punk'd* crew also appeared in *Cheaper By the Dozen* as Oprah's camera crew.)

Hilary also had a soft spot for co-star Tom Welling, whom she described as "so nice."

a cinderella story

Hilary's updated take on the classic Cinderella story delighted her fans upon its release. That's not bad for a centuries-old fairy tale—revisited, of course.

"*A Cinderella Story* is different. Sam's very independent," Hilary told the *Star Tribune*. "She's a plain Jane and she has a metamorphosis."

Indeed. Her ball gown is beautiful—albeit uncomfortable. (Hilary complained it weighed a lot and was difficult to wear.)

There was some difficulty nailing down an actor to play hunky (yet sensitive) quarterback Austin—Rupert Grint, who stars as Ron in the film series based on the popular Harry Potter books, was supposed to star in *A Cinderella Story* as Austin, but he had to drop out because of scheduling conflicts with *Harry Potter and the Prisoner of Azkaban*—but once Chad Michael Murray signed on, the cast was good to go.

Filmed in several areas of Los Angeles, the commute couldn't have been easier for Hilary—but her main reason for making the movie was because she liked the basic themes the plot had to offer.

"It's about high school and cliques and boyfriends and popularity," she says.

That sort of high school behind-your-back-stabbing seemed to be evident when critics took a stab at reviewing the film—Roger Ebert in the *Chicago Sun-Times* wrote "This is a lame, stupid movie ... sappy and dead in the water"; a *New York Post* reviewer said it was "an instantly forgettable wisp of marshmallow that revisits the same teen-crush clichés that have surely been in play since the days of the classic fairy tale it ransacks for inspiration." And perhaps worst of all, Stephen Hunter in the *Washington Post* said, "You can say of this movie, truly, that they took the most famous tale in the world and broke it."

The critics may not have loved it, but Hilary's fans seemed to—in its first two weeks the movie pulled in nearly $30 million.

And Hilary reached a new career high. Her *A Cinderella Story* salary was $2 million—twice what she got for *The Lizzie McGuire Movie*. That's some serious bank!

Hilary and Heather Locklear search for *The Perfect Man* next year.

Photo by James Devaney/WireImage.com

Coming Soon to a Theater Near You

RAISE YOUR VOICE

Hilary is sure to be a smash in this film, playing a girl who spends her summer at a performing arts high school in Los Angeles (think *Fame* meets *90210*). Hopefully that means she'll get to sing!

Set to open in theaters on October 9, 2004. this movie was originally going to

HILARY WANTED TO ACT EVEN AS A YOUNG KID "I JUST HAD THIS CRAZY DRIVE TO WORK," SHE SAID. "I STARTED DOING COMMERCIALS AND MODELING. THAT WAS PRETTY MUCH ALL YOU COULD DO IN TEXAS. I WAS BEGGING TO COME OUT TO CALIFORNIA AND TRY THIS OUT."

be called *Heart of Summer*. The film underwent some other changes early on—it was also allegedly going to star *Thirteen* actress Rachael Evan Wood—but luckily, Hils landed the part! The love interest, Jay, was also going to be played by Jonathan Jackson, but he dropped out due to production changes and was replaced with Oliver James (who played Amanda Bynes' love interest in *What a Girl Wants*.)

Hilary told *Billboard* her *Raise Your Voice* role has most likely been her favorite part yet.

"It's so dramatic," she said. "People really haven't seen me do this kind of role before. I play a character whose brother is dying." (Her brother in the film is played by Jason Ritter, who stars in *Joan of Arcadia* and is the son of late actor John Ritter.)

Also starring Rita Wilson and Rebecca De Mornay, the film will allow Hilary to show off some of her dramatic skills.

"I love the story; it's definitely more dramatic," she told the *Star-Tribune*. "It's kind of like a girl trying to find herself and she deals with a lot of stuff like her brother dying and it's her fault. It shows how she overcomes it, and she follows her dream and puts herself back together."

THE PERFECT MAN

In *The Perfect Man*, Hilary stars as a girl with matchmaking on the brain—she's trying to find her single mom the ideal boyfriend (but somehow ends up getting into more trouble than you can imagine!). Set for a spring, 2005 release, the movie recently finished filming (in Toronto and Brooklyn in New York), and Hilary couldn't be happier with the final results.

"*The Perfect Man* is a drama, and it's also very funny," she says. "It's a tearjerker with Heather Locklear and Christopher Noth. I loved working on it. A really cute script."

The film was directed by Mark Rosman, who helmed many of Hilary's *Lizzie McGuire* shows.

Wondering who to go see the movie with when it opens? Hils suggests taking your mom.

"It's a great mother/daughter movie," she told *Billboard*.

OUTWARD BLONDE

Hilary reportedly just signed on to this movie, said to involve a New York teen flunking gym and getting sent to learn to survive in nature (yikes!). No word from Hilary yet on whether or not she'll have to do any major stunts. ...

WHAT HAPPENED TO LIZZIE?

When *The Lizzie McGuire Movie* premiered, it was an instant hit; fans were sure many sequels would follow.

But that isn't exactly how things have played out. The Disney show was No. 1 in its timeslot during its two year run; it also inspired video games, toys and books. *The Lizzie McGuire Movie* made $40 million at the box office alone. And Hilary's two *Lizzie McGuire* soundtracks sold more than 2 million copies.

Fans loved Hilary's portrayal of the klutzy, cute, junior high every girl Lizzie McGuire. Yet still, Hilary and Disney pulled the plug on the show. Exactly how and when is up for debate. However, one thing is for sure, Lizzie will live on for years to come through re-runs—and through fan's memories.

SCREEN SCENE

Everything seemed fine while Hilary and the other Lizzie cast members were filming *The Lizzie McGuire Movie* in Italy (where Hilary reportedly ate for 11 days straight at the local Hard Rock—so often that they gave her a T-shirt). The days were long and the shoots intense, but Hilary seemed to be

Hilary has reportedly declined to film a (Lizzie Movie) sequel as of yet because of scheduling problems.

enjoying herself.

"It's been crazy the last few days, between shooting the movie, doing my school work on the set and trying to have some time for myself," she wrote in her online diary. "I have one more week left in Rome and I'm already excited to go to Vancouver [to film other parts of the movie]."

But the *Lizzie McGuire* phenomenon was about to end—at least for Hilary.

You wouldn't have guessed from the enthusiastic way Hilary was busily promoting *The Lizzie McGuire Movie* on talk shows and print outlets in the weeks preceding the film's release. She had never seemed happier with the role.

"I don't think I have outgrown the character because she is kind of grown up, especially in the movie," she said at the time. "The film shows her getting a little older. I may want to do other things here and there, but I don't think I'm growing out of this character."

Then suddenly came the news that there would be no more Lizzie. There were no plans for another movie and the show would stop production. Some outlets immediately blamed Hilary and her representation, saying they were demanding more money.

Not so, Hilary said—but she didn't mind taking a break.

"It's funny because the way it came out in the press was me leaving Disney because I wanted more money," she said. "That's not how it happened at all. All Disney Channel [contracts] are for 65 episodes at a time. We finished 65 episodes in two years, which is crazy. I was working in every single scene every single day; we worked straight through without any hiatuses. Even though I loved working on it, after a while it gets kind of tiring."

She tried to tell her fans that her motivations weren't monetary.

"It has been a very interesting week for me last week with all that crazy press out there," she wrote in her online diary. "It made me very sad to read some of your questions in regards if I'm only doing it for the money or if I'm getting greedy. Every Disney Channel show, from *Even Stevens* to *That's So Raven* and *Lizzie McGuire*, has only 65 episodes. Lizzie continues to be on the Disney Channel for a few more years and the decision about another Lizzie movie was not based on money, it had more to do with the working environment. I love being Lizzie and maybe there is another movie in the future."

Hilary has reportedly declined to film a sequel as of yet because of scheduling problems, but there may be one in the future. *Lizzie McGuire* is currently on the air daily (and in syndication on ABC Kids on Saturday mornings).

"Lizzie will be on the air two more years!" Hilary said. "The movie is on DVD. Lizzie isn't going anywhere. I just hope my fans like my upcoming projects as much as they did Lizzie."

There's no bad blood between Hilary and Disney. In fact, the company just released a new collection of songs called the *Lizzie McGuire Total Party*. The album also features three bonus karaoke tracks. It's sure to be a big seller—the TV show soundtrack certified platinum and *The Lizzie McGuire Movie* soundtrack is currently nearing double platinum.

Moving On

Hilary's no stranger to gossip, but fans thinking she had abandoned her star-making role really bummed her out.

In some ways, leaving the program was the best thing for the budding actress. *World Entertainment News Network* reported in July that she was almost relieved to see the show end because it had been such an emotional drain. Not only was the shooting schedule grueling, Hilary had begun to closely identify with her character.

"I was going through what Lizzie was going through—that teenager stage where you don't really know who you are," she said. "It was a good thing for me, but I worked my butt off. Everybody made a big deal out of it, like it was this horrible split."

Once again, Hilary stressed the positive side of the break-up.

"It got all blown out of proportion, like 'Hilary Duff and Disney split,' like this, that and the other, all these headlines about how I wanted more money to do a sequel or something," she says. "It wasn't about that. I wanted to do other things."

Sure, she'll miss many things about the Lizzie experience—but in the end, it was for the best, she said.

Where Are They Now?

Wondering what the rest of the *Lizzie McGuire* cast is up to? Here's an update on their careers ...

BFF Forever!

Lalaine Vergara-Paras (Miranda Sanchez) – Also known just as Lalaine, she played Lizzie's best friend on the show – and since has played characters in the 2003 TV movie *You Wish!* and the 2004 film *Promised Land*. Lalaine will also release an album later this year.

Buddy Boy

Adam Lamberg (Gordo) – recently filmed a movie called *When Do We Eat?* slated for a 2004 release.

Sibling Success

Jake Thomas (Matt McGuire) – Lizzie's little brother is graduating to some big roles in *Soccer Dog: European Cup* and *DinoCroc* (both to be released this year!)

Maybe Mom Needs A Break

Hallie Todd (Jo McGuire) – Hallie has kept a low profile since Lizzie ended, appearing only in the 2003 TV movie *Thanksgiving Family Reunion*.

Father Knows Best

Robert Carradine (Sam McGuire) – Lizzie's onscreen dad has been busy since the show wrapped, appearing in three films – *Comanche Stallion, Dreamweaver* and *Supercross*. All are due out in late 2004 and 2005.

© Warner Brothers/courtesy Everett Collection

"I love the cast and the crew and everything. We became like a family," Hilary said. "[But] it was time to do other things. When you do something for so long, it gets sort of repetitive."

Since stepping out of her Lizzie McGuire shoes, Hilary's kept busy recording a new album, touring and filming movies such as *A Perfect Man* and *Raise Your Voice*.

Still, she's aware some fans may have a hard time accepting her new, non-Lizzie screen persona. Hilary hopes her second, slightly different album will help show them a new side.

"The change might seem a little sudden because most people are used to seeing me as a character through Lizzie McGuire and movie roles that I played," she said. "So this music is a good way to get everyone to know the real me. Everyone evolves and changes."

Industry experts think Hilary will do just fine.

"I think she's definitely one of the hot people to watch right now, and I don't see that waning," Amy Doyle, vice president of music programming at MTV, told AP. "She's become the fabric of pop culture with teens right now."

And if fans slip and still call her Lizzie? Hilary doesn't mind a bit.

"It doesn't really bother me that people call me that," she says. "But my music is kind of what helps, I think, for people to get to know me better."

After all, she has Lizzie to thank. "That character really connected with people," she told the *London Free Press*. "It made it possible for me to pursue both a music career and an acting career."

AP Photo/Chris Pizzello

STYLE STAR

Funky shoes, bright lipstick and New Found Glory: they're just a few of Hilary Duff's fave items. The teen trendsetter has been known to rock some seriously cool looks, and her taste in music and movies is no less cutting-edge.

Check out some of Hil's top picks!

MUSIC

Like her own music—part pop and part rock—Hilary's taste in music is pretty diverse.

"I really like listening to [New Found Glory's] CD," Hilary said. "I have started getting into lots of different kinds of music. Now I like everything from Britney Spears to Eminem to 50 Cent."

Other recent CDs on Hilary's player? Rancid, Kanye West and MxPx. She recently also cited Maroon 5, Simple Plan, 50 Cent, Nelly Furtado and John Mayer as faves on her MTV music profile.

CLOTHES

Said to be a fan of Guess! and Bebe clothes, Hilary has been branching out lately. "I'm getting more into Los Angeles designers," Hilary said. A recent fave? Primp, an LA store featuring hand-knitted items and funky girl fashions. "Primp is feminine but also pretty hard-core, with knots and different fabrics."

She also likes to pop into LA store Tryst for some new duds. "This store has great clothes," Hilary says. And it's located on Ventura Boulevard in Studio City near another Hilary fashion favorite, Dari.

Like many L.A. stars, Hilary's also been known to stop by the super-trendy Kitson boutique. She and two pals were spotted on a shopping trip there for a 20-minute spending spree.

But Hilary doesn't dress up all the time—she recently arrived for a *Seventeen* cover shoot wearing a simple pink tank top and white miniskirt. (For the shoot she donned a Mimi & Coco tank and giant earrings by AHJewelry).

FANCY FOOTWEAR

"My favorites are Stella McCartney," she told *Teen People*. "I have so many shoes that we're having this service called California Closets build storage for them in our new house!"

She may be a self-confessed shoeaholic, but even Hilary sometimes opts for comfort over quirky fashion: At a recent Chicago concert, she wore just one outfit throughout the entire show—a black T-shirt, black skirt and Converse sneakers. Talk about low maintenance!

Hilary also likes the ballet shoe-esque, satin-lined Reebok Zenswas sneakers. Available in pink, silver and gray, they retail for $70 a pair.

BEAUTY BUZZ

Hilary says she never leaves home without Nars Chelsea Girls lip gloss. "I use it all the time," she says.

Hilary is also a fan of basic black eyeliner and mascara. "I carry it all in my handbag," she has said. "Luckily, all my bags are really big, because my entire life is in there!"

For before-bed face time, Hilary is a fan of Benefit's Pineapple Facial Polish, which sells for $24 a tube.

"No matter how good your skin is, no matter how tired you are, you have to wash your face every single morning and night," she insists. Of Benefit's Pineapple Facial Polish she says, "It exfoliates skin, too, so I make sure not to use it every day."

For the *A Cinderella Story* premiere, Hilary sported extensions, which were added for her new tour. ("for me to rock out on stage, I needed to get extensions," she said.) For the film premiere, her stylist straightened the extensions with a flat iron and makeup artist Rachel Goodwin added false eyelashes and fuchsia lips – a new look for Hilary!

According to Hilary, she's changing up her look from heavy black eye makeup to bright lipstick. "I'm really into my lips," she said.

FRESHENING UP

Hilary reportedly digs Mario Badescu Facial Spray ($12), which contains aloe. "It keeps skin really clean and fresh," she told Us Weekly.

ENTERTAINMENT

Hilary loved last year's Quentin Tarentino flick, *Kill Bill Vol. 1.* "I could watch this movie over and over again!" she said. "Uma Thurman had such control!"

She also raved about *How to Lose a Guy in Ten Days*. "It was so cute," she said. "Kate Hudson is amazing and Matthew McConaughey is so hot! I liked that."

She also digs Ace Ventura movies and other comedies.

"My sister, Haylie, and I love this movie!" she says of *Romy and Michele's High School Reunion*. "I love its message about rising above the negativism and jealousy."

On the small screen? Hilary's a reality girl. "I hate to admit it, but I do watch a lot of reality TV," she says. "I'm a big *Newlyweds* fan. I love *Fear Factor*."

Photo by Robin Platzer/FilmMagic.com

Hilary and skateboard legend, Tony Hawk attend the launch of Hasbro's Videonow Color Personal Player.

She is also an *American Idol* fan (who wanted Diana DeGarmo to win!) "I just think those girls and those guys who get up there are so brave," Hilary said. "I could never do something like that. I think they're really talented and I like the show a lot."

ACTING

Hilary loves the challenge. "When I'm singing, I feel like I'm totally myself. When I'm acting, it's a little harder," she said. "I have to kinda put myself in somebody else's shoes."

CLEVER GUYS

"I don't like guys who look like they spend more time in front of the mirror than I do," she told agirlsworld.com. "They have to be smart. That's important, but it so hard to find guys because I'm always working!"

EATS

Hilary's been very vocal about her favorite restaurant, the star-studded sushi spot, Nobu.

"Every time I'm in New York city, I treat myself and go to my favorite restaurant, Nobu," she said. "I'm a big sushi fan! It's great."

But sometimes healthy fare just won't do it – at a recent photo shoot she requested pizza be ordered for lunch.

CHILLING OUT

Hilary relaxes by jumping on a trampoline in her backyard. She also likes to listen to loud music to unwind.

How does she beat bouts of sadness? Hilary either goes for a swim or reads one of the *Chicken Soup for the Soul* books. "I'll be reading one of those, and I'll either laugh hysterically or start bawling," she has said.

HOT SPOTS

Hilary loves hanging out at coffeehouses (she's often been photographed out and about with a giant cup in her hand!) and at the beach.

ANIMALS

An avid animal lover, Hilary owns a dog and also adores horses—she even chatted about her equestrian obsession in a recent issue of Cowboys & Indians magazine!

PAL POSSE

Hilary said her role in *A Cinderella Story* was a hard one because she couldn't

HILARY'S ONE FASHION FAUX PAS? "I TRY NOT TO WEAR SUNGLASSES," SHE SAYS. "BECAUSE IF YOU SEE SOMEONE WHO WALKS INTO A ROOM WITH SUNGLASSES, AREN'T YOU GOING TO LOOK AT THEM AND THINK, WHO'S HIDING UNDER THAT? SO WHY WOULD YOU DO THAT?"

Photo by S.Sarac/Everett Collection

Call her devoted but Hil knows her fans put her where she is today. If she stops to sign one autograph she's likely to sign 20.

relate to the character's loner life. Hilary makes spending time with friends a priority and often brings some on tour with her. And when she can't have them tag along, there's always the phone. "I love to text message," she says.

TRAVEL TREA

Hilary's favorite travel kit is said to be the Bellezza Box, which contains a shower pouf and six Principessa beauty/skin care products. It's designed to pamper the "urban princess."

MEETING FANS

She loves it—but it can get overwhelming. "Usually if I sign one autograph, I end up signing at least 20," Hilary said. "It's hard, because I have so much support from all those people and it's because of them that I get to do what I love to do every day. Usually, the only time I don't sign an autograph is when I'm literally running away because there's a big crowd or something. But even when I'm running, sometimes I'll yell back to them, 'I'm sorry!'"

AP Photo/Chris Pizzello

Still to come

Think Hilary's fashion line and entertainment achievements are all she has planned? Think again – 'cause Hilary's not done yet!

Hilary Duff certainly has packed a lot into the past 16 years – from her childhood in Texas, to acting in L.A., to rising to superstardom in the movie and music industry, she seems to have done it all.

But for a workaholic like Hilary, this is just the beginning.

"I work really hard," she says. "I take my job really seriously."

But not too seriously. When questioned by a reporter about the reaction to her summer blockbuster *A Cinderella Story*, Hilary waxed philosophic.

"I know that the critics didn't love it," she said. "I pretty much got good reviews; it was the script that they didn't mostly like. That's fine with me. Everyone can have his own opinion. I think I have a great fan base. "

"I'm not sure what the opening numbers were; I don't want to know. I never want to know that stuff. I have a great team around me that helps me do great things every single day."

These days, that can be a lot. "There's always stress involved," Hilary says of her schedule. "I never have five minutes. If I'm not on set shooting a scene, I'm either in hair or makeup, changing my clothes, doing a phone interview real fast, having a meeting, or working on lines."

"Being on tour, I'll be doing meet-and-greets [with fans] or doing radio interviews or going here. It's a different kind of busy. It's all a lot of fun. But after a while it starts to get pretty stressful. I've stopped asking; I just show up, and they tell me what to do — and I do it."

Stage and Screen

With two films on the way—*Raise Your Voice*, slated for October, 2004, and *A Perfect Man*, set for a February 2005 release - Hilary will be no stranger to moviegoers.

She's excited about her *Raise Your Voice* role.

"It's so dramatic," she told Billboard. "People really haven't seen me do this kind of role before."

They have, however, seen her pack her schedule to include filming two movies and recording an album at once. Some fans have recently expressed concern about Hil's busy agenda, but the actress has no complaints.

"I'm working 'round the clock," she said. "No summer vacation. But it's fun!"

Between touring to build excitement for her new album before it's fall release and shooting, Hilary's torn between her two great loves—acting and singing.

"You feel a very accomplished, rewarding feeling when you finish a movie and you're like, 'Ok, I did it.' But the singing definitely gives you more energy," she said. "When I'm on tour, I'm in a new city every single night, and the energy, the crowds, the kids screaming and knowing every single word of my music, and being onstage is such an energetic feeling."

"Sometimes, if I'm in the middle of touring, I'll be like, man, I really wish that I was working on a movie right now. Or if I'm working on a movie, I'll be like, oh, I wish that I was touring right now. I just love them both so much."

Music Matters

"People say, 'Oh she's an actress, and now she thinks she's a singer. What a joke!' Or you get people writing horrible reviews about your CD," Hilary said. "I really didn't have that much support in the beginning. The radio didn't start playing my music until they started seeing how well my albums sold, and it was really the fans that did that."

Her 20-plus city tour was a hit with fans—and with Hilary.

"When you're on stage and you have a sold-out venue of 15,000 people and they all know every single word to your songs and they're holding up huge signs and freaking out, it's just like: 'Oh, my God!'" she says. "The support you're getting from them and the energy!"

Hilary's music has been a summer hit, including her *Our Lips Are Sealed* cover, recorded with sis Haylie. The song landed in the Top 40, and its accompanying video

Photo by Debra L Rothenberg/FilmMagic.com

was one of MTV's top-10 videos in June, 2004.

Hilary's next album is due out on September 28, 2004.

"I'm so pumped up about [the new album]," she has said. "It's so different than the first one. The sound is much more mature. And I got to write a lot of it."

Yet Hilary promises her new album won't alienate her younger fans.

"I don't think that it is too mature that kids couldn't listen to it. I just think that other people will relate better," she says.

Her debut album, *Metamorphosis*, landed the No. 2 spot on the Billboard 200 in its first week of release; the first single off the album, "So Yesterday," was an instant radio hit and TRL video staple.

"I've always sung, ever since I could talk," said Hilary. "At home, at school, in the choir, everywhere. But about two years ago I decided to be a real singer, and started working with really cool singers, musicians and songwriters. Best of all, I started working in the studio, experimenting and putting material together. I've really fallen in love with the studio."

Feeling Famous

Hilary is well-known—but for a reason.

"I work my butt off," Hilary has said. The results are obvious—she has a huge fan base, a burgeoning music career and several movies on the way.

"I feel lucky, very lucky, all the time," said Hilary.

"Not a lot has changed in the four years since I first worked with her," Mark Rosman, director of *A Cinderella Story* and *Lizzie McGuire* said. "She's still incredibly sweet and grounded. She could be the model for being a successful teen star who's still a real teen."

He says that while she may seem to be a savvy businesswoman, Hilary's still a teen at heart.

"She still laughs at the same things that other 16-year-olds laugh at, and she doesn't get certain things that only adults get. I find that refreshing for someone who's so successful," he said.

In her free time, Hilary also continues to work with charities, especially "Kids With A Cause", a group that helps children suffering from poverty, hunger, sickness, lack of education, abandonment, neglect and/or abuse. Hilary has worked with "Kids With A Cause" since 1999. Haylie Duff is also involved (she was the organization's 2003 spokesperson!).

And although Hilary recently finished her high school studies, someday, she'd like to be a student again.

"College is something I want to do down the road," she has said.

That seems like a lot for one person to take on—higher education mixed with super stardom. But for Hilary? No big deal. She'll undoubtedly be a successful at both.

"I'm very ambitious, and I'm very driven," she said. "I don't know where that comes from, but it's always been there. Now that I've achieved some stuff and I'm getting to do all these wonderful things, I'm not satisfied. I want to keep pushing myself."

Photo by Scott Gries/Getty Images

Photo by George Pimentel/WireImage.com